This Book Belongs To:

FB

4.3/1.0
NO AL

SEBASTIAN
(Super Sleuth)
and the
Santa Claus
Caper

Other books about Sebastian

Sebastian (Super Sleuth) and the
Hair of the Dog Mystery
Sebastian (Super Sleuth) and the
Crummy Yummies Caper
Sebastian (Super Sleuth) and the
Bone to Pick Mystery
Sebastian (Super Sleuth) and the
Secret of the Skewered Skier

MARY BLOUNT CHRISTIAN

SEBASTIAN
(Super Sleuth)
and the
Santa Claus
Caper

ILLUSTRATED BY LISA McCUE

Macmillan Publishing Company
New York

Collier Macmillan Publishers
London

Macmillan Publishing Company
866 Third Avenue, New York, N.Y. 10022
Collier Macmillan Canada, Inc.
Printed in the United States of America
10 9 8 7 6 5 4 3 2 1

Library of Congress Cataloging in Publication Data
Christian, Mary Blount.
Sebastian (super sleuth) and the Santa Claus caper.
(Sebastian, super sleuth)
Summary: Dog detective Sebastian goes undercover
as Santa Claus to unravel a mystery at a department
store.
[1. Dogs—Fiction.   2. Mystery and detective stories.
3. Christmas—Fiction]   I. McCue, Lisa, ill.
II. Title.   III. Series: Christian, Mary Blount.
Sebastian, super sleuth.
PZ7.C4528Sep   1984   [Fic]   84-4424
ISBN 0-02-718460-9

Remembering George D. Blount,
my father, my friend, my fortress

Contents

1

Who Was That Jolly Fat Man?

Sebastian scrunched down—*oof!*—and peered under John's bed. Nothing there but lint balls, one dirty sock, and a rubber squeaky toy. Maybe John was getting better at hiding things. But John—Detective John Quincy Jones of the City Police Department—needn't think he could outsmart the greatest dog detective in the world!

Sebastian shimmied into the closet, leaving the door open a crack. He dug among the shoes and assorted junk. Not there, either. Could it be that John hadn't bought it yet? It was only a week until Christmas—just six more shopping days.

Surely John wasn't going to wait until the last minute and settle for some slipshod token of a gift for him! Hadn't the old hairy hawkshaw served faithfully and grandly on the police force with John since puppyhood?

1

Although John was the only official detective—that is, the only one actually *paid* for his services—it was he, Sebastian (Super Sleuth), who sniffed his way through clue after clue until the criminals were brought to justice. Didn't he, therefore, deserve a super present?

Suddenly the closet door was opened wide, and Sebastian found himself face to face with his human.

"Good grief!" John said, obviously startled. "What are you doing in the closet, old fellow? You aren't burying one of your bones in there, are you?"

Sebastian shot an accusing look at John. How could he forget to buy a Christmas present for his canine confidant, his fantastic partner through mystery after mystery?

John pulled his overcoat from a hanger. He put on his wool cap and gloves. "Got to pick up the paycheck, old fellow. I need to get some Christmas shopping done today. But I'll take you for a run in the park later."

Big deal! Sebastian thought. A run in the park. His pads freezing off in the snow, while he romped around like an ordinary dog.

Then Sebastian's ears perked up. Paycheck? Shopping? Of course! John had been waiting for his Christmas check—probably so he could get something especially nice. Sebastian wagged his stub of a tail enthusiastically and gave his human a warm, friendly lick on the hand.

John chuckled. "I think I'll take you to the station with me. Chief gets so riled up when he sees you that he forgets to bawl me out for whatever he thinks I did."

Sebastian sighed. Was that all his company meant to John? A buffer between him and the chief? Well, at least it would get him out of that small apartment for a while. Let the chief bring on his roughest insults. Sebastian the long suffering could take it.

Sebastian certainly shared his human's apprehension about facing Chief. What a grumpy man! Still, there was always just compensation. Sebastian could count on Chief to have some gourmet goodie—a danish roll, an eclair, or sometimes a sandwich and fries—tucked away in the office for sneaky snacks.

Chief was forever on a diet—probably one reason for his mean attitude! Instead of eating in the open, he hid the goodies and ate when no one was looking. Sebastian felt he was actually helping Chief by getting rid of those nasty temptations. He licked his whiskers in anticipation of a treat.

The snow sent icy chills through Sebastian as he

trotted to the car beside John and leaped in. He only hoped that Chief wouldn't give John another case to invesigate. It was, after all, their day off, and John did need the time to find the perfect Christmas present for his fuzzy partner.

At the station John stuck his head through the doorway of Chief's office. "Sorry to bother you, Chief," John said. "But I came to pick up my paycheck. I'll just grab it and get out of your wa—"

"Nonsense, my boy," Chief said. He pushed his mouth into an unfamiliar smile. "Come in and sit down, er, John. And bring your fine dog, too."

Cautiously, suspiciously, Sebastian edged into the office with John. "Fine dog"? What had happened to "walking flea trap" and "four-legged garbage disposal"? This was a side of Chief the old sleuth had never seen before, and he didn't trust it. What kind of game was Chief playing?

Chief walked around to the front of his desk and patted Sebastian on the head. Then he leaned back on the desk, facing John. "Tell me, my boy. How is your lovely mother?"

"F-fine, sir," John replied. He shifted in the chair, drumming his fingers on the arm. He was obviously confused by Chief's new manner, too.

"Did—did you want to see me about something in particular, Chief? I mean, if it's about that plant in the lobby that Sebastian—"

4

Chief smiled again. It was such an atypical look that Sebastian found himself staring, fascinated.

"No, no—heh, heh—doggies occasionally get frisky. In a few years it'll recover and look like the rare and expensive plant it is. No, I just don't ever get a real chance to chat with you. And this being the *Christmas* season, the season of *sharing* and all that, I wanted to make the time."

John shifted again. "Thank you, sir. That's very kind of you."

Sebasian caught the scent of a jellied waffle on Chief's desk and edged closer, still following the conversation.

Chief folded his arms with a sigh. "Er, speaking of your mother, are you, er, eating Christmas dinner with her?"

"I spent Thanksgiving with my mother," John said. "And since I have to work the day before and the day after Christmas, there won't be time to go all the way home. I guess it's just Sebastian and me and the turkey."

Sebastian licked his lips. A turkey for him! But what would John eat?

"Of course," John added, blushing, "my girl friend and I plan on a little gathering for a few friends in the evening, so the day won't be a total loss."

Urrrrr. Sebastian curled his lip and groaned.

5

John hadn't said anything to him about Maude Culpepper and entertaining that evening. He'd planned on a quiet evening—without that woman and her flirty dog. At least there would be dinner alone!

Chief sighed mournfully. "My wife is visiting her sister in Canada. The first Christmas in years. I'm thrilled for her, but that does leave me at loose ends." He sighed. "*Alone*, all, all alone for Christmas —except for Meemew, that is."

How awful! Sebastian thought. Alone on Christmas with a—a *cat*!

"I would like to stop by your place on Christmas, my boy," Chief said. "I wouldn't want to interfere with your celebration, but I want to bring you and, er, what's-his-name a little something."

He was fishing for a dinner invitation! That old sneak! Sebastian slipped over to the waffle and in one slurp—goodness, the jelly made it slippery!— swallowed it.

Sebastian caught a glimpse of the *real* Chief for a moment, as a quick scowl clouded the man's face and he opened his mouth to yell. But somehow Chief managed to turn his yell into a chuckle. "Dogs will be dogs. Don't worry about it, John, my boy."

John grabbed his paycheck with one hand and the fur on Sebastian's nape with the other. "Er, we'd better be going, sir. I'm sorry. We—goodbye, sir."

"Would noon be convenient?" Chief called after him.

"N-noon, sir?" John stammered.

"To come by with your Christmas gift."

John flushed. "Oh, er, sure, sir. Thank you."

Sebastian trotted out to the car. Gift, indeed. He was trying to trick John into inviting him and that stupid cat to dinner.

"Chief was sure in an odd mood today," John muttered, as he shifted the car into gear and eased into the traffic. "I don't think I ever saw him that friendly before. I wonder what got into him. He said he has a little something he wants to give me. What could it be? Now I suppose I'll have to get him a present, too."

John maneuvered the little car around a stalled eighteen-wheeler, still muttering. "If it's a *little* something, I'd better be careful not to outdo him. Wouldn't want it to look as if I were trying to get on the boss's good side. Or have him think I'm earning too much money and not give me a raise. On the other hand, I don't want to look cheap and ungrateful. I don't know what to do."

Sebastian knew what to do. Lock the door and pull the curtains shut, and maybe Chief would

7

think they were gone. That was all they needed—
to have Chief come and bring that dumb cat with
him.

At the bank Sebastian anxiously counted the
money John withheld from his deposit. Would it be
enough to buy an appropriate gift for a roommate,
detective partner, and all-around good dog?

Sebastian wiggled excitedly and pressed his nose
to the cold window, watching as John slowly inched
his way through the snarl of cars. He planned his
strategy. He'd pretend to be interested in the store
displays and the other shoppers. He would hang
back a little in the store so John would feel free to

browse for the best possible present for the clever canine. He'd stay just close enough to peek, but not close enough to intimidate his human.

The car groaned to a stop. Sebastian squinted to see through the fogged window. That wasn't the mall! That was their own apartment. Surely John wasn't going to leave him—

John reached over to tousle Sebastian's fur. "Sorry, old fellow. Can't go shopping with me, boy. No dogs allowed in the mall."

Sebastian crouched in the car seat, whimpering. No peeking? No subtle herding of John into the right departments, to the right counters? No fair!

Sebastian, hangdog, slunk into the apartment, drawing apologies from John. You have to keep humans in line, after all! But as soon as John left, Sebastian broke into a panting grin. Did John really think he could fool the cunning canine that easily? Surely he just wanted to be alone so he could buy Sebastian's present.

Sebastian couldn't help himself; he had to know what John was getting him for Christmas. So the curious canine pushed open the doggie door and galloped at full speed through the flurries of snow toward the neighborhood mall. Sebastian (Super Sleuth) was hot on the trail!

2
Dashing Through the Snow

John had mentioned the neighborhood shopping mall, so Sebastian headed in that direction. Cars jammed the streets, bumper to bumper, their windshield wipers slapping at the snow flurries, their exhaust misting like dragon's breath. Sebastian figured he'd reach the mall by the time John got there and found a parking place, even with the head start he had.

The mall seemed ablaze with color and lights. At nearly all the entrances, bells tinkled as costumed people urged shoppers to drop money into their charity kettles. Christmas music blared from every store, but each song was different, so they all jumbled together in a mishmash of noise.

Sebastian dodged the booted feet of the passersby and scooted toward the door of Cheatum's department store. Since Cheatum's was known for its fine merchandise, surely it would be John's first stop.

Sebastian skidded to a stop at the door. His eye was caught by a bold sign: NO FOOD OR DRINKS INSIDE. NO DOGS ALLOWED, SEEING EYE DOGS ONLY. *Humpt!* he thought. And they called themselves a classy store!

A woman wrapped in a fuzzy coat, muffler, and stocking cap led a group of children to the entrance. Dressed in plush parkas, snow boots, and mittens, the children looked like a litter of sheepdog puppies, tumbling and pushing along behind her.

"Hurry up, now," the woman commanded, waving a gloved hand. "Everyone join hands so you won't get separated and lost in the store. And don't touch anything, or you won't get to talk to Santa Claus. Is that clear?"

Furry hoods bobbed in answer. "Come on, now," the woman said, shoving Sebastian into the line. "I said everyone—no exceptions!"

Eagerly Sebastian got into line. If the woman thought his fur was a parka, fine! It saved him the trouble of creating a disguise, as masterful as he was at such things. He'd been a maitre d', a gypsy, and an airline attendant. He figured he could be a kid at least long enough to get inside the store.

The woolly line of children, including one clever

chameleon canine, wove through the aisles, following the red arrows toward the toy department and their final destination—Santa Claus's castle. Occasionally a mittened hand reached out toward something on the counters, but as soon as the woman yelled, the hand retreated.

When one hand retreated too quickly and sent a bottle of perfume crashing to the floor, Sebastian used the distraction to slip away unnoticed. He skittered through the legs of the shoppers and ran toward the Slumber Shop.

Perhaps John was going to get him a silky soft comforter for the cold nights ahead—Sebastian had hinted for one often enough, snuggling under John's blanket until John ran him off. Or a Sebastian-size four-poster bed like one he'd seen in the Christmas catalog. The store called it "The Pampered Pooch." He'd prefer something a little more macho, of course, but he wouldn't exchange it—that would be rude.

Sebastian scoured the Slumber Shop, but he couldn't find John.

"There's a dog loose in here!" one of the clerks shrieked. "Get security!"

Sebastian scooted across the aisle, into the camping department, and inside a tent. He skidded into someone. The old hairy hawkshaw held his breath and stared gloomily at the stranger's sneakers. He figured the stranger would yell for the guards and turn him in.

But to his surprise, the stranger just tugged his rumpled raincoat up around his chin and pulled his fedora so low that only his handlebar moustache showed. He dipped his head so Sebastian couldn't get a good look at him and exited hastily, muttering an apology.

Puzzled but relieved, Sebastian peeked through the tent flap and saw several security people rushing up and down the aisles.

While he waited for the excitement to die down,

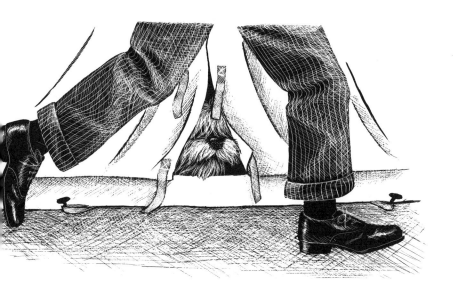

he looked around to see if there were any gift possibilities in that department. A barbecue pit, perhaps? John knew how much he loved barbecued steaks and roasts. Maybe that was what he was getting him.

When he heard the security people assuring the saleswoman that she had not seen a dog at all, Sebastian darted out of the tent and searched for John. He spotted him in the jewelry department.

Oh, dear, Sebastian thought. Maybe John was getting him a jewel-studded collar. That would be so tacky. A sterling silver water bowl engraved with his initials (or perhaps a replica of his family crest) would be nice, however. He peered through the legs of the shoppers and strained to hear John's conversation above the noise of the loudspeakers.

"A music box, I think. Maybe something by Brahms," John was saying.

A music box! What on earth was John thinking about? Why would the old super sleuth want a music box? Especially one that played Brahms! If John wanted to get him something musical, why not a stereo? And a couple of records by Dave Brubeck? Cool jazz—that was more to his personal, exquisite taste. Or maybe some rock and roll by The Who. But Brahms?

"My mother has always loved Brahms," John

told the saleswoman. "I think she'd like Brahms's 'Lullaby'."

His mother? Sebastian growled under his breath. He supposed it was fitting that a man buy his mother's present first. He only hoped John didn't spend so much money on her gift that he didn't have any left over for the old sleuth!

"And let me see that while I'm here," John said, pointing.

Sebastian stretched his neck, trying to get a better view. A gold, engraved identification tag, maybe? Not that he, Sebastian (Super Sleuth), was the type to get lost. But a bit of gold at the neck can be quite dashing and contemporary.

"Gift wrap it, please," John said. "In paper appropriate for a young single woman."

Humpt! Sebastian groaned. Single woman, indeed. He was probably getting something for that Maude Culpepper. Sebastian had known she'd be trouble from the moment John's mother had introduced them—her and that dog of hers! How *could* John think of her before his faithful companion?

"A dog! I told you there was a dog in here!" A high-pitched shriek reached his ears.

The security guards shoved through the crowd, yelling above the sound of "Silver Bells," which came from the loudspeaker. "There it is! Get it!"

Sebastian scampered across the floor, dodging feet and the arms that grabbed for him. He turned a corner and pushed through a door that said EMPLOYEES ONLY. DO NOT ENTER.

Sebastian skidded to a halt, staring.

On a bench in front of some scruffy metal lockers lay Santa Claus! He had a cloth over his eyes and was groaning and muttering to himself. "It's inhuman. Nobody should have to go through such torture. I just can't take it anymore."

Sebastian shrank into the shadows as Santa Claus suddenly sat bolt upright, pulling the cloth from his eyes. "I won't take it anymore. Let 'em get someone else!" He yanked off the red cap and threw it on the bench. "I'll go back to my old job as lion tamer—it's safer!" With that he pulled off the beard and wig. He tugged at the buttons on the coat, and several pillows fell to the floor.

Why, it wasn't the real Santa Claus at all! Sebastian concluded. It was only one of those store helpers.

The man left the Santa Claus costume in a jumble on the bench. He pulled his clothes from a locker, dressed, and left, laughing hysterically.

Before the door swooshed shut, Sebastian caught a glimpse of the security guards, who were still running about looking for him. If they found him,

John might be so angry that he'd forget Sebastian's Christmas present altogether, and that wouldn't do at all!

If he was going to get out of the store without being spotted, he was going to have to use a disguise. Of course, if he could find that group of children again, he might not have to come up with anything. As his own lovable self, he'd fooled the woman into letting him join them before. But it might be hours before that group left the store. Besides, he prided himself on his disguises and welcomed the opportunity to create a new one.

Sebastian sank to the floor and scratched his ear vigorously. *Mmmmmm.* It had to be something spectacular, but what? His eyes fell on the discarded Santa Claus costume. That was it! Their personalities were a great deal alike, after all. They were both generous, handsome, and modest. He'd be a natural!

Easily Sebastian scrambled into the Santa Claus suit. He'd just wiggled into the hat when the door to the lounge burst open and a man with a flower in his lapel yelled.

"There you are! We've been looking all over for you. A big bunch of kids are waiting to see you, and they're getting rowdy! We told them you were feeding your reindeer, but that's not going to hold them

for long. Now, get out there before they tear up the whole toy department!"

Sebastian nodded. He'd have to go along with this for a little while, anyway. He trotted out the door and turned right.

"Not that way!" the man shouted. "This is the last time I'll hire an out-of-work lion tamer!"

Sebastian, looking hangdog, followed the man toward the toy department. He was halfway there, when suddenly water burst from above.

Shoppers and clerks alike screamed, pushing their way to the outside doors. It was the overhead sprinklers.

"Fire!" someone shouted. "There must be a fire!"

18

3
Here Comes Santa Claus!

As people yelled and shoved toward the exits, Sebastian sniffed the air. He smelled perfume and leather and wet wool. But he didn't smell smoke.

"Don't panic!" a voice over the intercom insisted. "We're sure it's only a false alarm. Please wait at the entrance. We'll cut the cost on merchandise as soon as we reopen in a few—"

"Watkins, are you crazy?" a gruff voice interrupted. "We don't want to mark down the price. People are willing to pay more at Christmas, so let 'em."

"Sir, the microphone is open. Are you sure you want to say this now?"

"Er—heh, heh—ten percent off wet merchandise, ladies and gentlemen. Cheatum's won't be undersold," the second voice said. "Watkins, see me in my office at the end of the day," it added.

Whatever had set off the sprinklers had automatically triggered the call to the fire station. Within minutes firefighters appeared, their hoses at the ready.

John juggled his packages to one side and flashed his badge. He urged the customers to come to order. "Please," he said. "If you shove, someone will get hurt, and there are lots of little kids in the crowd today. You wouldn't want to hurt them, would you? Now, be calm, please."

A man wearing a dark blue suit and a worried look wiggled a finger at John, motioning for him to come. Sebastian, who was nearby, eased close enough to hear, too.

"I'm the owner—Horace Cheatum's the name— and I think someone deliberately set off the sprinklers to hurt my business." It was the same gruff voice Sebastian had heard over the loudspeaker.

"Then you should tell the police," John said, shifting his packages to his other arm.

"I just did!" Horace Cheatum said.

"Uh, of course, sir," John said, blushing slightly. "It's just that this is my day off and—"

John melted beneath Mr. Cheatum's glare. "Well, I can always shop in the evenings, after work," he said, sighing wearily. He adjusted his packages under his arm and scrounged in his pocket for his notebook and pencil. "Now, what makes you think this wasn't just a freak accident?"

"Well, for one thing," Mr. Cheatum said, "this isn't the first embarrassing, store-stopping thing that has happened."

"Do you have any ideas about who might be causing the 'accidents'?" John asked. "Or why?"

"Pah!" Mr. Cheatum said. "It could be anyone—my competitors, my employees, a dissatisfied customer. Nobody likes me. You have to be tough in business, and you make enemies. The better you are, the more enemies you have. And I'm very good."

Mr. Cheatum scowled at Sebastian, who was still in the Santa Claus costume. "The emergency is over. I'm not paying you to lollygag around the store, you know."

Growling under his breath, Sebastian trotted toward the toy department. It was a good thing he wasn't the *real* Santa Claus. Mr. Cheatum would get nothing but switches and ashes in *his* stocking Christmas morning!

Sebastian decided it would be a good idea to stick with his disguise for a while. It might give him a chance to investigate the incidents undercover, and it would keep John from finding out he'd come to the shopping mall. Besides, he couldn't disappoint the kiddies!

He felt wet and uncomfortable, and he was hungry, too. Fortunately he had to pass the store restaurant on the way to the toy department. He spotted several half-eaten ham-and-cheese sandwiches on a table near the door.

Sebastian swooped them up and swallowed. Soggy, but not bad. He trotted to Santa's throne and plopped down. Already a line of children was waiting.

A plump woman in a red and green costume was cooing at the children. "Hi, there, kiddies! I'm Merry Christmas, and I'll take your picture with Santa Claus. But you have to quit hitting and shoving now. You know, Santa's making a list and he's checking it twice!"

She leaned toward Sebastian, whispering. "If old Cheatum doesn't start paying me better, he can take this job—Hi there, dearie," she said to the little girl who was first in line. "Come on up and tell old Santa what you want for Christmas."

As the little girl made her way up the steep steps to the throne, the woman whispered again. "Would you believe that I'm old Cheatum's secretary? It's just so humiliating to do this, year after year." She clicked her tongue against her teeth. "See?" she said to the girl with corkscrew curls. "I told you Santa had to go feed his reindeer, and now he's back. Go on, Tracey." She shoved the girl, who was wearing a nametag.

Tracey edged closer, eyeing Sebastian cautiously.

"Go on," the woman urged. "Be nice, or Santa won't come to see you. Smile for the picture now."

The girl stood eye to eye with Sebastian. She narrowed her eyes to slits. "You don't look anything like Santa Claus, anyway," she said. "And you smell like my dog Toby after he fell in the creek!"

She reached up and pulled on Sebastian's fur.

Errrrrrow. He growled deep in his throat and narrowed his eyes, too.

Tracey's eyes popped open. "It's a real beard! You really are Santa Claus! Wow! I want a video game and a doll that cries and cowboy boots and a dump truck. You don't need to bring my baby brother anything, 'cause he'd only break it, anyway."

The girl rattled on, and Sebastian muttered a low *mmmmmmm*, nodding his head as she spoke. Then he grasped a lollipop between his teeth and shoved it at her. And satisfied, she left, slurping noisily on the candy.

Merry Christmas motioned for the next one to come.

A boy stalked up and kicked Sebastian on the knee. *Oof!* "You forgot the racing track last year," he growled. He shoved a foot-long list toward Sebastian. "This year I wrote it all down, so you won't have no excuses."

Ummmmmmmmm, Sebastian replied, shoving a

24

lollipop toward the boy's eager hands. Poor Santa Claus! Sebastian thought. Did he have to put up with this every year? No wonder he had helpers!

Sebastian hurried through the rest of the children on line as quickly as possible. After all, he was a detective first, Santa Claus second. And he had to get on with his investigation. John would be lost without him. Besides, the quicker he solved the case for John, the sooner his human could get back to Christmas shopping.

Sebastian (Super Sleuth) would discover who was sabotaging Cheatum's department store and put the culprit in Chief's stocking in time for Christmas!

He trotted away from the throne, only vaguely aware of a red lollipop that was stuck to his fur.

4
He's Making a List and Checking It Twice

The first thing to do, Sebastian decided, was to make a list of all the suspects and check them out. He broke into a panting grin. Santa Claus was right. Make a list and check it twice!

His tummy rumbled. Dogs cannot live by lollipops and ham-and-cheese sandwiches alone. If he was going to think straight, he had to get some life-sustaining food—pizza, hamburgers, or what have you.

He found the employees' cafeteria and got in line. Immediately he recognized the figure in front of him. It was the stranger in the fedora, sneakers, and raincoat whom Sebastian had surprised earlier in the tent.

He sniffed. Was that grease paint he smelled? As a connoisseur of disguises, he certainly recognized a bad one when he saw it. But why was the stranger in disguise? Was he a store detective working undercover? If so, why hadn't he called the security guards and reported a dog in the store?

Puzzled, he nosed his tray along, as the people behind the counter piled a plate high with baked chicken, mashed potatoes and gravy, green beans, and custard and a steamy cup of hot cocoa for dessert.

A young woman followed close behind. "Is it fun talking to those little kids all day?" she asked Sebastian, taking his mind off the stranger in disguise.

He whimpered.

"Really?" she asked. "At least you get to sit in one place all day. I mean, they put me in the ceramic shop, and every time I move I'm scared to death I'll break something. All that expensive stuff sitting around."

Mmmmmmm, Sebastian replied.

"That'll be a dollar ninety-five," the cashier told Sebastian.

He stared at her. He had to *pay* for it? But he had worked all day for free. It wasn't fair. He howled softly. *Oooooo.*

"Hey," the woman behind him said. "No sweat. It's on me, Santa. I mean, what's money, after all? I'd rather it went for somebody's food than for broken ceramics, huh?"

He nodded gratefully and carried his tray to a table. The young woman followed.

"Working here is such a drag, isn't it? I mean, that old Cheatum is worse than Scrooge! He'll figure out a way to make his employees pay for that discount on the wet merchandise, I'll bet. And you can believe he keeps us after work to do the inventory—without paying extra for it."

Sebastian slurped the gravy and wolfed down the chicken. And because he was extra hungry, he ate even the green beans. They weren't bad, once he'd dipped them in the gravy. He gobbled up his custard, pausing only long enough to nod occasionally to the young woman, who talked constantly.

After all, he owed her something—she *did* buy his meal for him. Besides, he figured, some of the information she was giving out might prove valuable, once he'd had a chance to digest it—and his meal!

"And giving us only five percent off the store price for things we buy here. Rotten! Most stores give twenty percent to their employees and still make a profit. And he fired the manager, his own nephew. Can you imagine? Said the guy was too easy on the employees!"

Sebastian made a mental note to make Cheatum's nephew his first suspect. Had he determined to get even with his uncle for firing him? Sebastian nodded his thanks to the young woman and rose.

She waved cheerily. "You're a great listener," she said. "There aren't many good listeners in the world anymore." She glanced around, then leaned forward, whispering, "But, frankly, your table manners are for the dogs."

Sebastian shot her a hurt look, then snatched up his cup and trotted off. He planned to finish his cocoa on the way.

No sooner had Sebastian downed the last drop of cocoa than—*clunk!*—a passerby dropped a quarter into the cup. She must have thought he was a roving charity collector!

Hmmmmm. If others thought so, too, he, Sebastian (Super Sleuth), would be able to wander freely about the shopping center. And he'd have this case cracked quicker than eight tiny reindeer could pull a sled full of toys! That would leave him free for more important work—like finding out what John was buying him for Christmas!

5

What to His Wondering Eyes Should Appear?

"Harrrumph!" A gruff voice snapped behind Sebastian. He whirled to see if he'd been caught once more. But the noise had been directed at one of the sales clerks, and it had come from Mr. Cheatum, who was walking up and down the aisles like a general at post inspection.

John was following Mr. Cheatum, trying to balance his packages and his notebook and take notes as he walked.

"If you don't have a customer at the moment, don't just stand around gawking," Mr. Cheatum scolded the woman. "Dust!"

"B-but I've already dusted!" she protested, flustered.

"Then dust again!" he said. "Busy, busy, busy!"

Clink! Someone else dropped a few coins into Sebastian's cup. He nodded gratefully.

"I started as a clerk myself," Mr. Cheatum said

to John. "Never knew what a day off was. Still don't. These idlers'll never get ahead, never get ahead. Lazy, lazy."

It did seem to Sebastian that as Mr. Cheatum passed each station, the clerks burst into a flurry of activity that dwindled as soon as he was out of sight. They certainly were afraid of him!

"You said this wasn't the first store-stopping incident, that there have been others. What sort of sabotage are we talking about, Mr. Cheatum?" John asked.

"There was the morning we found molasses in the shoes—that was six weeks ago. And four weeks ago the wires on the lamps in the lighting department were snipped so that none of them worked. And then two weeks ago we found the china cups glued to the saucers. And last week someone painted moustaches on all the mannequins."

Troublesome, Sebastian concluded. But not your dangerous criminal type.

"Those sound like childish pranks," John said. "Have you made anyone mad lately, in the last six weeks or so?"

"Constantly!" Mr. Cheatum said. "When you work like I do, you—"

"Make people mad," John finished, nodding. "But has anyone threatened you?"

Mr. Cheatum rubbed his chin briskly in thought.

"You know I'm in big competition with Gerald Ripov. His store sells the same merchandise and is in this mall. He cut prices to the bare bone, trying to run me out of business. He even took a loss, I'm sure of it. But it didn't work. I matched him penny for penny. He's a jerk, even if he is my brother-in-law!"

"Your brother-in-law?" John gasped. "You mean that Ripov, your biggest competitor, is your brother-in-law?"

"I just said that, didn't I? Must I repeat myself constantly? Repetition is costly, young man."

John blushed. "S-sorry, sir. It's just that it seems a bit strange that you're in competition with your brother-in-law."

"Wouldn't have been if he hadn't been such a sore loser," Mr. Cheatum said.

"I don't think I understand," John said.

Mr. Cheatum waved John off and approached the floorwalker. "Don't just stand around with your hands in your pockets! You're a floorwalker. So walk! How else can you keep these people working for their money? Do your job or leave!"

"But, Father!" the floorwalker said.

"Father"? Sebastian's jaw dropped. The floorwalker was Mr. Cheatum's own son, and he was threatening to fire him!

"Harumph!" Mr. Cheatum said. "At the store,

I'm Mr. Cheatum. Don't be familiar with me."

"Yes, F— Mr. Cheatum." The man stalked off, his face red.

Good grief! Sebastian thought. Now there were two more suspects to add to his list—Mr. Ripov and Mr. Cheatum's own son!

Mr. Cheatum suddenly whirled, facing Sebastian. "You needn't think that just because you are following me, I'm going to drop anything into that cup! I gave at the office!"

Sebastian resisted the urge to nip Mr. Cheatum on the ankle. He hung back, trying to look inconspicuous. He'd have to be more careful of Mr. Cheatum from now on.

"I'll talk to your brother-in-law, of course," John said. "But maybe you'd like to tell me what you meant when you said he was a sore loser."

Mr. Cheatum bent to stare at several brass candlesticks on display. Frowning, he snapped his fingers and pointed to them. Immediately the clerk rushed over with a dustcloth and wiped them. Satisfied, Mr. Cheatum moved on.

"I mean that I won out as chairman of the board of this store and eventually became the owner, and he just couldn't stand working for me. He moved down the mall and started his own store, using his father's money."

Mr. Cheatum held his head up in a superior man-

ner that irritated Sebastian. He'd be interested in getting Mr. Ripov's version of the story!

"'You mentioned that your employees might have done this. They'd have the opportunity," John said. "But do they have a motive?"

"I suppose they get a bit upset when they have to really *work* for their money," Mr. Cheatum said. "But I don't want any freeloaders in my store. I fire those who don't stand up to the job at hand. Maybe some of those fired might want to get even with me."

Sebastian curled his lip in distaste. He could add to that list of suspects anyone who had ever met the man. To know him was to dislike him—a lot!

"If I can go through your personnel files," John said, "perhaps I can get this case closed quickly."

And get back to Christmas shopping! Sebastian thought.

"My secretary should be back in my office by now," Mr. Cheatum said. "She has been doing some er, ah, volunteer work."

Some volunteer work! Sebastian grumbled. That man had her doubling as Merry Christmas down in the Santa Claus castle! Sebastian made a mental note to add her to his list of suspects. Beneath that Christmas spirit was one angry woman!

Was she angry enough to sabotage the store?

6
There Arose Such a Clatter

Sebastian trotted toward the office as close behind John and Mr. Cheatum as he dared. He wanted a good look at those personnel files, too. If they held a clue to the vandalism, he, Sebastian (Super Sleuth) would spot it right away.

"Oh, look, dear," a woman said. "It's Santa Claus. Give him a big kiss so he'll bring you lots of toys." She shoved a baby toward Sebastian. "Kiss, kiss!"

The baby socked Sebastian with a rattle and screamed like a banshee. The woman pulled the baby back and shrugged apologetically. "We'll see you next year," she said, dropping a few coins into his cup.

Not if he saw them first! Sebastian hurried toward the back of the store. He had to get out of that Santa costume. It was just too hazardous!

He spotted a door that said MAINTENANCE and

pushed it. Inside the room, hanging on a hook, were coveralls and a cap. On the bench nearby was a tool belt. They would do nicely. Sebastian left the Santa costume and the collection cup on the bench and changed clothes.

Moments later Sebastian (Superintendent) emerged and headed for the office. He trotted in and ambled past the outer office, where John sat with the secretary. He went directly into Mr. Cheatum's office.

Sebastian examined the desk immediately. It was empty, except for a picture of a woman about Mr. Cheatum's age. It must be Mr. Cheatum's wife, the sister of Gerald Ripov, owner of the competing store. The picture was signed, "Love, Ima."

Sebastian broke into a panting grin. Her name was Ima Ripov Cheatum! If that wasn't motive enough—

"Maintenance!" the secretary snapped, startling Sebastian. "It's *my* desk, not Mr. Cheatum's, that needs repairing. Out here!"

Sebastian trotted into the outer office, where John was going through the files with the secretary. Her real name, it turned out, was not Merry Christmas at all but Sara Brewer.

Sebastian crawled under the desk, clutching a hammer between his teeth. *Tap, tap.* He hit the

underside of the desk gently, so that he would seem busy but would not drown out the conversation.

Ms. Brewer pulled a file. "This is Clem Emory, who was fired about the same time all the sabotage started," she said. "Six feet two, dark hair, green eyes—quite a hunk, actually. He worked in the furniture department. Mr. Cheatum caught him taking an extra twenty minutes for lunch one day and fired him." She sighed. "Mr. Cheatum wants everyone to be as dedicated to the store as he is."

Sebastian figured you could disguise a lot of things with costumes. But you couldn't hide that much height. He thought of the stranger in the fedora. Certainly *he* was nowhere near that height. John could be wasting his time investigating this Clem Emory. Then again, maybe the stranger in the fedora was only a shopper with bad taste and not a culprit in disguise.

Maybe Clem Emory was angry enough at being fired to try to get even with Mr. Cheatum. Still, Sebastian didn't feel that Emory was his man, and he trusted his instincts. They'd never failed the clever canine before! Well, almost never.

"Isn't it getting awfully hot in here?" John asked Ms. Brewer, interrupting Sebastian's thought.

Sebastian had to admit that he himself was panting.

Ms. Brewer wiped the sweat beads from above her lip. She leaned over, peering at Sebastian, who was still under the desk. "Maintenance, go check, will you? Something must be wrong with the furnace. It feels like the tropics in here."

Sebastian didn't want to miss any conversation, but he had to stick with his disguise. He nodded and left, the tools clattering as he trotted toward the basement.

Mr. Cheatum rushed up to him. "You've got to do something! Customers are deserting the store in droves! The heat is unbearable!"

Sebastian pushed open the door to the stairwell and came face to face with the stranger in the fedora. The man had just come up the steps from the basement.

Sebastian watched him pass and was tempted to follow the stranger. Now he was sure that somehow the man was mixed up in the sabotage. But first he had to tend to the heat.

He found the thermostat right next to a sign that said, SAVE STORE MONEY. KEEP AT 68° IN WINTER AND 72° IN SUMMER. The glass cover that had been placed on the thermostat to keep people from accidentally resetting it was broken. Shattered glass lay strewn about the floor.

Gingerly Sebastian stepped over the glass to get

a closer look. The thermostat was set at 95°—high enough to send people dressed in their heavy winter wools scurrying out of Cheatum's and to the competition. Obviously the change in temperature was no accident. And Sebastian knew the stranger in the fedora had something to do with it.

But who was the stranger? And what was his motive?

The hairy hawkshaw turned the thermostat back down to 68°. Then he trotted upstairs, hoping to catch sight of the mysterious stranger.

He was in luck! The rumpled raincoat was just disappearing through the crowd, moving toward the exit. Sebastian scooted after him, the tools clanging against his sides. It was certainly easier for a maintenance man to clear a path than it was for Santa Claus.

Sebastian kept just a few feet behind the stranger and followed him right to Ripov's department store. Maybe Mr. Cheatum was right! Maybe it *was* his brother-in-law! Maybe the man was trying to get even with Mr. Cheatum for taking over the store.

The stranger was moving faster now, and Sebastian loped to keep up. He raced into a hallway and around the corner, past the arrow that said REST-ROOMS AND EXECUTIVE OFFICES.

The stranger was nowhere in sight. Sebastian pushed through the door marked MEN. The restroom was empty! Sebastian scratched his ear, thinking. He hadn't been that far behind the man. Where could the stranger have disappeared to?

7
... Laughing All the Way

It dawned on Sebastian. If the stranger had come down that hall but wasn't in the men's restroom, then either he was in the executive offices—or he wasn't a *he* at all. Could he be a *she*?

Sebastian bounded out into the hallway and leaned casually against the wall, trying to look like a maintenance man on a break. He kept his eye on the door to the women's restroom. Would the stranger come out?

He waited, watching. A young woman came out, holding the hand of a toddler. Then a woman with grayish blue eyes and gray hair, toting several large shopping bags, came out and turned toward the executive offices. Her face looked vaguely familiar. Two other women followed, carrying sacks of wrapped packages. Sebastian waited a little longer, but no other women came out. Satisfied that the stranger was not in there, Sebastian trotted down to the executive offices. Suddenly the door marked GERALD RIPOV, PRESIDENT, swung open, and a man and a woman walked out, arm in arm.

She was the older woman with the large shopping bags, whom Sebastian had seen moments before. The man, now carrying the shopping bags, had the same grayish blue eyes and gray hair. If that was Gerald Ripov, the woman must be his sister! It was Mr. Cheatum's wife, Ima.

Sebastian bent over and pretended to be hammering the carpet into place. He cocked one ear.

"I have tried everything I know to convince Horace to sell the store to me," Mr. Ripov said. "You'd think all these strange incidents would persuade him to retire."

The woman patted his arm. "I'm still holding onto those two cruise tickets to Hawaii. Surely he'll give in soon."

Sebastian gasped. They were in it together! He'd been causing all those "accidents," trying to convince Mr. Cheatum to sell out. And Cheatum's own wife knew! She'd even arranged to take Cheatum to Hawaii—to get him out of the way—while Ripov took over. He never thought he'd feel sorry for that mean old Mr. Cheatum. But, poor man, he was the victim of a conspiracy!

The cagey canine glanced into the shopping bag as Mr. Ripov passed him. In it were sneakers, a raincoat, a fedora, and a phony moustache!

"Do come back and see me, sister dear," Mr. Ripov said. "And next time we see each other, I hope we are celebrating the merger of Ripov and Cheatum department stores, or at least the permanent retirement of Horace Cheatum!"

They disappeared around the corner. Sebastian loped in that direction, hoping to keep them in sight. Just as he rounded the corner, he nearly ran into Mr. Ripov, who was returning to his office. He was no longer carrying the shopping bags. Had he stashed them somewhere in the store? Had he given them to his sister to hide?

How could Sebastian prove that Mr. Ripov was the stranger in the fedora when he couldn't speak the human language? It would take John forever to come to the same conclusion. And without the expert eyewitness testimony of Sebastian (Super Sleuth), John wouldn't have a case. This was a real challenge for the old hairy hawkshaw!

But Sebastian would figure out a way. He dog-trotted to Cheatum's department store.

When he arrived, he ran right into the weirdest scene yet! The entire storeful of people had the giggles, absolutely hysterical laughing fits. Tears welled in the eyes of customers and clerks, who yucked, sniggered, and guffawed.

What was going on? Sebastian wondered. Then his sensitive nose told him—laughing gas, the stuff dentists used to make people open their mouths wide. He spotted John and Mr. Cheatum running around, waving their arms.

"This—ha, ha—is horrible!" Mr. Cheatum said. "You've—heh, heh—got to do something! I'll be ruined—ha, ha."

The gas was coming through the air vents. Already several maintenance people were heading for the control center in the basement. They'd have the gas stopped and blown out in no time. Sebastian was more concerned with how the laughing gas had gotten there in the first place.

Sebastian wasn't much affected by the gas, because he was so low to the ground. Sometimes walking on all fours had its advantages.

Suddenly Sebastian spotted the fedora. Mr. Ripov must know a short cut to the store! If he could just catch the man and unmask him in front of John and Mr. Cheatum . . . . Sebastian made one heroic leap, knocking Mr. Ripov to the floor.

The felt hat tumbled to the floor, revealing the culprit.

But it was not Mr. Ripov at all! It was Mrs. Cheatum!

"Poopsie!" Mr. Cheatum said. "Ha, ha. Wh—heh, heh—what are you doing here—and in that ridiculous outfit?"

Sebastian pulled himself up. "Poopsie"?

"Snuggles. Ha, ha," Mrs. Cheatum said. "I-I'm so ashamed. Heh, heh."

Sebastian looked from one to the other. "Poopsie"? "Snuggles"?

"You—ha, ha—you mean that you—? Heh, heh. The molasses? The glue? Ha, ha. The heat? You?" Mr. Cheatum helped her up. "But why?"

Mrs. Cheatum giggled. "Because sometimes I think you care more about this store than about me. Ha, ha. I thought I could convince you to sell out or to pass it on to our son—he is a responsible adult—heh, heh. You're always promising to go to Hawaii with me, and I'm tired of taking second honeymoons alone. It's—ha, ha—just not the same!"

"Heh, heh," Mr. Cheatum said, helping to brush the dust off his wife. "But—but I had no idea! I'm only working hard for you!"

Mrs. Cheatum hugged him. "Then stop it," she said. "I don't want it. I want my Snuggles again."

John blushed. "Er—ha, ha. Can I assume, sir, that this case is closed now? Heh, heh."

Mr. Cheatum grinned sheepishly. "Yes, thank

48

you. And from now on, so is my office. It's time I gave that son of ours a chance to manage this store. He can give his uncle Gerald a run for his money, don't you think so, Poopsie?"

Mrs. Cheatum smiled and blushed. "Anything you say, Snuggles."

Sebastian sniffed. The maintenance people had successfully flushed out the laughing gas. The store seemed back to normal. He wiggled out of his disguise and shoved the tools and coveralls behind a counter. If he didn't get out of there fast, he was going to be sick from an overdose of sweet! Snuggles and Poopsie, indeed!

Sebastian trotted home, content that John had returned to his Christmas shopping. He settled back for a dognap, with visions of sugarplums dancing in his head.

Now that the minor mystery had been solved—what was John getting him for Christmas?

8
The Stockings Were Hung...

John spent the remaining days before Christmas on routine police work, too boring for Sebastian's interest, and shopping for presents.

Although he brought gifts to the apartment each evening, to Sebastian's chagrin, none of them supported nametags. Did John suspect that he knew how to read? None of them had particularly intriguing scents, either, although the curious canine sniffed them, one and all. Sebastian would just have to wait for Christmas to find out what John was getting him.

John put up their stockings and decorated the tree on Christmas Eve. He hung the gingerbread men and candy canes. Sebastian helped as best he could.

"Nine, ten, eleven . . ." John counted. "Now I could have sworn I put up twelve." He counted again. "Eight, nine, ten, e— Sebastian! Are you eating those gingerbread men?"

Sebastian gulped, swallowing one cookie whole. They were too tempting, although he did try to temper his appetite for them by alternating with candy canes.

"Well," John said, chuckling and stroking Sebastian under the chin. "Christmas comes but once a year, old fellow. Although you really should cut down on the calories, I guess it won't hurt to gorge yourself this once."

Sebastian was grateful for John's change of heart—so grateful that by the time John had awakened on Christmas morning, the tree was minus both candy canes and gingerbread men as high as Sebastian could reach. He did wish John hadn't put away the ladder!

By eleven o'clock, the tantalizing smell of roasting turkey and dressing teased Sebastian's nostrils. His tummy rumbled. But the real reason he was anxious to finish with the meal was that only then would John allow the presents to be opened.

John dressed Sebastian in a red and green plaid bowtie and a white bib that looked like a tuxedo front. He chuckled. "You look rather dashing in costume, old fellow. You should wear clothes more often!"

Sebastian turned his head to hide the smirk on his face. If only John knew . . . .

The doorbell rang at precisely noon, just as John was removing the turkey from the oven. It was Chief. He was standing in the doorway with a package in one hand and that stupid cat Meemew in the other.

"Ho, ho, ho!" Chief said. "I—I didn't interrupt your dinner, did I?" He craned his neck around the doorjamb and sniffed. "Mmmmm, something sure smells good."

"Come in, Chief," John said, to Sebastian's dismay. "Sebastian and I were just about to have Christmas dinner. Why don't you and Meemew join us—if you don't have any other plans, that is."

Chief stuck the package under the tree and sat down at the table. "Good job on that department store vandalism, John. Strange case!"

John got another plate, silverware, and napkin, and lit the candles. "Thank you, Chief. The poor lady just got tired of waiting for her husband to retire. She figured she could trick him into it, I suppose. Turns out her brother didn't have an inkling of what she was up to.

"If it hadn't been for that unidentified maintenance man not looking where he was going, the case would have taken me a lot longer to solve. He, of course, accidentally knocked her down, causing her disguise to fall off. And he became frightened and ran away."

Sebastian scowled. Accidentally knocked her down? Frightened? When would he ever get the kind of gratitude he truly deserved?

John filled plates for Sebastian and Meemew. Then he and Chief ate. Sebastian ate his food, then part of that finnicky cat's, enduring her incessant purring and rubbing as best he could.

Meemew rubbed against John and purred noisily.

The flatterer! Sebastian thought, curling his lip. He nosed her aside and licked John's hand. She wasn't going to get ahead of him!

When the dishes were done and the meal was only a lovely memory, they all gathered around the tree.

Sebastian wiggled in anticipation. First John handed Chief his present. It was a desk set made out of phony leather. Sebastian twitched anxiously. Next John handed a small package to that stupid cat. She tore into it, uncovering a bag of catnip.

"Open mine!" Chief said. "I can hardly wait for your reaction."

John tore open the package that Chief had brought. Sebastian stared in disbelief.

It was a framed picture of Chief and Meemew.

Ick! Maybe it would make a good dart board!

Chief grinned broadly. "Well, what do you say? Are you surprised?"

John gestured nervously. "What can I say? Surprised isn't the word, Chief."

Chief leaned back, obviously satisfied. "I knew you'd like it."

Sebastian stuck his cold nose into John's neck. What about his present? Why didn't John hurry?

"Here you go, old man," John said. "I hope you like it."

Sebastian sniffed. Too small for a barbecue pit and too big for a gift certificate at the meat market. What could it be?

Eagerly Sebastian tore into his package. A rubber bone? A bone? Rubber? He'd waited 365 days from last Christmas for a *rubber bone*? For that he'd followed John to the mall and solved another case for him at the risk of his own life and limb?

Sebastian sighed a long martyr's sigh. Oh well, he thought. His present to John would be pretending he was a regular chase-and-fetch kind of dog. It just might be his best disguise ever.

Anyway, Christmas was only one day, and he could pretend for that long. But criminals beware:

Tomorrow Sebastian (Super Sleuth) would be back
on the job.

Sebastian tossed the bone into the air, then
pounced on it, urging John to join in the chase.
After all, 'twas the season, and all that good stuff.